SEEK TO BARE

Seeking in Romance Book 3

KEKE RENÉE

304 Publishing Company

INTRODUCTION

Are you signed up for my newsletter?

Join today and find out all the latest in new releases, contests, giveaways, sneak peeks and more.

https://BookHip.com/ZXCKSSF

DISCLAIMER

THIS WORK OF FICTION contains strong language and explicit sexual content and is only intended for mature readers. This story may contain unconventional situations, language, and sexual encounters that may offend some readers. I would recommend selecting another book. This book is for mature readers (18+).

SYNOPSIS

Kyla worked hard to make her Hollywood dreams come true. She wanted the roles and the opportunity to do what she loves. What she never expected was how quickly she would lose her right to privacy and safety. Unfortunately, she learns that lesson in a frightening way when a delusional stalker sets his sights on her.

It was the man she couldn't forget after a one-night stand in Vegas who came to her rescue in more ways than one. She will need Warren to help her, but will she be held back by her past? Neither could've anticipated it would blow up in their faces.

The Weekend in Vegas.

"How much are you going to put on her, Morris?" Kyla asked, laughing at Morris. My girl came out with me to Vegas so I could have company while he worked with Warren. We'd already gone shopping and then gambling, so we ended up at the pool in our bikinis, laying under the sun. Chelsey and Maya had to work and FaceTimed us earlier. Next time they're free, we'd all fly out together.

"As much as I think she needs," Morris grunted, and I chuckled as they went back and forth like brother and sister. He was a perfect gentleman and didn't allow me to pay for anything when we arrived, and he had us in the suite for the entire weekend.

"He hasn't taken his hands off you since we've been out here," Kyla said, sipping her margarita.

"Kyla, leave him alone." I laughed at the scowl on his face.

"Oh, calm down, crazy man. You've run all the guys away," Kyla fussed, and he kissed my forehead.

"Good," he said.

"Morris, I got Barry on the phone wanting to talk to you." I glanced up as Warren approached us.

"Hi, Warren," I said.

"What's up, brat?" he teased, nudging me playfully.

Morris stood, took the phone out of Warren's hand, and stepped near the empty cabana for privacy.

"Kyla, you remember Warren, right?" I introduced them as they stared at each other.

"Ummm... Hey," Kyla said.

"What's up?" Warren responded and went to walk toward Morris.

"What was that?" I asked.

"Huh."

"You two just eye fucked each other," I whispered.

"Lisa, please," Kyla chortled.

"I'm just saying we're here for the weekend—nothing wrong with a one-night stand."

"No thank you. Men and relationships are not on my agenda," Kyla explained.

I raised a glass, Kyla picked up hers, and we toasted.

"Then maybe you should try out Club Seek when we get back."

"Hmmm..."

"The best place to be." I laughed, took a sip of my drink, and watched my man talk with his friend. I thought of all the fun we would have later that night.

KYLA

F*lashback: Vegas*

I bit down on my bottom lip as the rope tightened around my wrists; I couldn't explain why I agreed to this besides showing him I wouldn't flake on him, that I could go with the flow. All we'd done this whole time in Vegas was stare at each other throughout the night; something about him intrigued me. The only problem was making sure nothing leaked out, and we promised each other this was a one-time thing. Soon as it was over, we would act like strangers once again and ignore each other. I noticed the thick muscles of his arms and couldn't wait to have them wrapped around my body. The suitcase on the floor held different intricacies, and I got to pick which one to use. Lisa told me this weekend was about being spontaneous, and taking her up on the offer would come in many rewards.

"Kyla."

"Huh."

"Shit, you're already leaking, baby."

"Warren..." *I felt the push of his finger entering my awaiting canal. He moved the flogger across my thigh gently.*

"Who made you drip like this, baby?"

"You did... Ahhhh!"

He picked the whip up next and went across my inner thigh. The growl he muttered beside me somehow made the scene more intense. Was I really doing this? Kyla Stevens, actress and daughter of Abigail Stevens, the well-known baker in my hometown was about to indulge in a one-night stand with a man while he performed a BDSM scene with me.

৩৯৩

I RELEASED THE LAST BREATH I HELD AND FELT THE bright lights against my left cheek, as the director called action on set. Today was a quick scene of me doing the opening act of my character finding out she needed to get closer with her mother. I'd been wanting this role for a while and as an established actress, getting the meaty type of film parts where you were stripped of all the glitz and glamour came sparingly. Lately, my mind had been distracted by the little situation I had in Vegas. Living in Tennessee for a limited time to complete the project kept me busy and stressed at times. For today, it would be me and one other actor on set, but in two days, I would need to do press, try to film two more long scenes, and clean my rental place before my cousin came to visit. I'd dreamt of this life, but the only way to ease the tension at times and the demand was to join Club Seek. Lisa told me how she was introduced to the club as a place where she could go without any judgement, to escape the day-to-day life choices.

"Kyla, let's try that again. I need more emotions," the director ranted, making me want to throw in the towel and call it a day.

"Can I have a minute?" I asked.

He shot me a look. "Five minutes."

"Thanks." I tightened my robe, went over to the actor's chair, and sat, closing my eyes and running a hand across the back of my neck.

"Guess who." Two hands covered my eyes, and I cuffed both wrists, shaking my head.

"Not sure. Is this my best friend who I forgot to call back yesterday?"

"Correct." Lisa dropped her hands and stepped in front of my chair.

"You look cute today."

"I had a good night's sleep," she teased, biting on her index finger. I grinned, tapping her on the butt.

"I bet you did."

"Kyla, we're ready for you." The assistant director approached me.

"Thanks, Brandon. Lisa, you don't mind waiting, do you?"

"No, go be the star that you are."

"Great, it's a small scene." I hugged her, heading back to set. I sat on the couch, lifting the photo in my hands.

"Quiet on set please. Kyla, make sure you remember what I said," Tevin said, stepping behind the monitor to watch the scene. I cleared my throat, focusing on the photo and concentrating on the goal of the character in the moment.

"Action!" he yelled.

"All I ever wanted was your love. Why did you do this to me!" I slammed the photo down on the table and covered my face as I cried.

"Cut! That's it for today," Tevin informed me.

I jumped up and strolled over to the monitor, looking at the playback of myself.

"Keep pulling those types of emotions, and we're good." Tevin pushed the headphones toward me to listen.

"Thanks, Tevin."

An hour later, I drove over to meet up with my friends. I stopped at the stop sign and swiped up on my cell to see a new email notification. My agent was working on trying to get another sit-down for a huge film with me as the lead.

"Please be the one," I mumbled underneath my breath, clicked into my email, and my lip twisted up in disgust.

Unknown: We know about Vegas.

"What the fuck."

Bark! Bark!

A car horn went off behind me, and I ignored it, trying to respond, and closed out to pull back on the road. Ten minutes later I arrived at the restaurant a little frazzled.

I was sitting with Lisa and Chelsey at London's restaurant and bar, wearing black shades, sitting in the back near the inside of the booth. I took every precaution when going out to avoid being harassed by photographers.

"What have you been up to, Chelsey?" Lisa questioned.

"Working at the bank as usual, focused on family." Chelsey placed her fork down and wiped the residue of the mustard from the corner of her mouth.

"Did you tell her about Vegas?" Lisa asked.

"No, and I thought we promised not to speak on that."

"What happened?" Chelsey questioned, her face squinted in concern.

"Can I tell her?"

I waved her off; nobody could stop her from talking. Not even Morris. She smirked, sipping her wine.

"Fine, she hooked up with Warren in Vegas."

"Warren... Morris' business partner?" Chelsey asked.

"A one-time thing, not a big deal."

"Only because you're on this career path, forget your personal life," Lisa blasted me in front of Chelsey.

"You have your career, same as Maya and Chelsey. Why is it a problem for me?"

"Because that's all you think about." Lisa rolled her eyes. It's been over a year since I met the rest of the women after Lisa introduced us. We'd met because of an interview she did with me, and our friendship blossomed from there. Sometimes she could be a little overbearing with trying to boss everybody around.

"Not true, but the men I've seen aren't used to my lifestyle."

"Have you gone to Club Seek yet?"

"No."

"You need an escape; you've done the Vegas thing. Now try something that will get your inhibitions going," Lisa teased, bumping me on the shoulder.

"Unlike you and Maya, my public persona would get run through the mud."

"Stop worrying about what people think about you."

"Can we change the subject?" I dropped my fork on the table.

Lisa lifted the bottle of wine and filled our glasses.

"One night, and then I'll shut up about it." Lisa held her hand up.

"Why do I have a feeling this is going to backfire?"

Chelsey sat back and crossed her arms over her chest, pushing her breasts up and revealing her silk blouse. I was surprised Xavier didn't say anything about her walking out of the house with one.

"One night, Lisa, and nothing more."

I decided on a nude silk dress that showed just enough cleavage, with a small gold necklace and black heels with a key shape on the back. The crowd was packed inside, and I shouldn't have been surprised since Lisa told me the weekends were the most popular. I followed behind Lisa as her plus one since Maya and Chelsey had other plans tonight. I'd wrapped up filming and went straight to Lisa's place to get changed, and Morris had a car waiting to bring us to the club. Mason had the place secluded and mysterious with it being away from other businesses and sitting as a stand-alone location.

"Did I tell you every man in here is watching you?" Lisa turned with a huge smile and passed a martini toward me. The bartender didn't charge her for the drinks and said everything was on the house, according to Mason.

"Thanks. I didn't know what to expect, so I wanted to be classy, but sexy at the same time."

"No worries, babe. You're making a huge impact on all the guys tonight."

"They have shows up front, but if you like to watch privately, it can be arranged."

"I'm fine right here." I took another sip of my drink.

Right as I started to speak, my mouth shut, and my body tingled at seeing him again so soon without warning. I would hope Lisa didn't set me up, but something told me it wasn't an afterthought he'd be here. This man knew what he did to women, the small curve of his upper lip as his tongue grazed his teeth. Remembering how well he kept his dreads neat, sides freshly shaved as I pushed my hands through them, I gulped down the rest of the drink, cursing myself for thinking about the way he had me calling out his name over and over again, while he hovered over my back. Soon as I went to order a second drink, I smelled his cologne getting stronger, which meant he was getting closer.

"Warren, I didn't know you'd be here," Lisa said, a slight smirk spread over her face.

"What's going on, Lisa? Your boy didn't tell you I was coming?" Warren replied, never taking his eyes off me.

"I must have forgotten. You remember my friend Kyla," Lisa responded, taking the drink out of my hand.

"I was still drinking that." I pouted, placing my hands on my hips.

"Warren can order you another one. I need to see Morris." Lisa waved goodbye, and I felt duped for even thinking she'd be my wingman.

"You look disappointed?"

"I have no reason to be disappointed."

"Glad to hear that." He pulled on his beard.

"What is that supposed to mean?" My eyes narrowed in a glare.

Warren's eyebrows hiked up, and he grinned.

"Lil mamma, that feisty attitude won't work on me."

"Warren, please, you're not God's gift to every woman."

"I don't need to be. Only one woman will get this gift." He walked up on me and closed the space between us. I tried to take a step back, but he closed both hands against the bar on either side of me.

"Warren, you want a drink?" the bartender interrupted our stare off.

"I'm good. You want anything?" he responded, stepped back, and put a space between us. A part of me liked the closeness and protectiveness he provided.

"Uh... No... No," I muttered low under my breath.

"Great, because tonight I want you fully open to what I'm going to do your body."

"Huh."

"Did you enjoy what we did in Vegas?"

"Yeah..."

"Do you want to explore those moments again, Miss Stevens?"

"Okay."

"Then come with me." He took my hand and led the way out of the club's main entrance and through the private section. My thoughts ran all over the place at what he'd be doing to my body tonight. A part of my brain said to just turn around and act like this never happened, but I wanted to be Kyla and not the superstar actress everyone looked at as simple and cute. I could be bold, daring, and outgoing with my choices in life, but I always thought that would lead me to a path that would hinder my career. Warren went to the front of a private door that held a sign in gold plate labeled Restricted.

"Are we supposed to be in this room?" I asked.

He slid a key in, turned the knob, escorted me inside, and shut the door behind me.

"For high-priority guests," Warren said, removing his

jacket and laying it on the back of the door. Warren turned the lights down low from the wall, picked up a remote from the side table, and I scanned the room in surprise. The palace was huge and unexpected for a club, but Mason was well known and rich. The colors were fire red, and the bed was raised off the floor with long drapes hanging; it was more of a Victorian or Greek style. I saw a door in the corner that more than likely led to a bathroom, so I walked off to gather my bearings.

"I'm doing this," I whispered to myself. I looked in the mirror and felt my face to make sure I wouldn't pass out or anything.

"It's just sex."

"Kyla?" I heard his raspy voice.

"Coming right out."

I shook off my nerves. The last time I was this nervous, I was losing my virginity at seventeen and believed I was in love with my high school boyfriend. Blowing out a long breath, I left the bathroom and stopped in my tracks. Warren stood completely naked, and I wasn't sure if his dick grew even more since Vegas, or I was that gone off his sex that I let something that big inside me.

"Uhm."

"Strip." He held up a pair of handcuffs in his hand.

"Warren."

"I can fulfill your needs, Kyla, but you have to let me, baby."

"Have you always been that big?" I extended my hand, dramatically forming what I thought was his size, and he laughed, causing his dick to jump.

"Come over here."

I followed him toward the bed and dropped my dress, only wearing a red thong set, and kicked my heels off.

Warren lay on the bed and locked his right hand in the handcuffs to the side of the headboard.

"What are you doing?"

"I want you to take the lead. Go at your speed."

"So, like you're my sex toy?" I giggled, not believing him.

"Just for the start, and then I run the show." He motioned for me to come closer, and I noticed the piercing on his shaft. I scanned from the top of his head to his beautiful brown skin against the bright red colors in the room. My mouth was ready to take him down my throat and show him how much I could please him. I wasn't just a timid lover.

WARREN

I watched as she crawled to me on the bed, wearing the sexy red thong set she wore under her dress. Our first adventure in Vegas sparked a fire in me to want to be around her all the time. She probably thought the first time we met was in Vegas, but I'd seen her with Lisa when Morris had to stop over to see her. The Vegas trip was the first time we actually spoke, and I thought she'd be some uptight bougie actress that would think I was beneath her or something. Watching her come up to my chest, she planted a trail of kisses and ran her tongue over my pierced nipple.

"Show me what you can do, Miss Stevens."

My right hand caressed her arm, moved to the back of her head, and yanked her closer to me, deepening our kiss. Out of all the women I'd been with, they never had me moaning, but Kyla brought the best upfront. Kyla leaned back and pushed her chest in my face. I slipped my tongue across her breasts, gripping her ass, and buried my face in her chest. Cuffing myself to the bed was a good idea at first, but not being able to fully hold her pissed me off. Kyla sat over my lap, stretched her hand back, squeezed, and grazed her fingernail gently over the tip.

"Warren... Warren... can I taste you?"

My breathing increased, and my eyes twitched when she scooted back and took him down her throat in one swift motion.

"Fuck!"

I jerked my hand, forgetting I was wearing handcuffs, trying to touch her while she watched me. She was teasing me, sticking her tongue out, then spat on my tip, and sucked me back in her mouth.

"Ssshhhittt." I gritted my teeth.

Her head went up and down quickly, then stopped and moaned.

"That's enough," I grumbled, reaching for the key from the table.

Kyla smiled and released me before I came. I pushed her on her back, swiped my tongue over her sex, still covered in her thong. Palming her breasts, I lifted her legs up, removed her bra and underwear, and nuzzled my nose in her sweet honey. I nibbled on her inner thigh and plunged a finger in her core.

"Awww!" she gasped, closing her eyes. I flicked my tongue over her warm sex, feeling her juices pour down my throat. Kyla would be thinking of me only from here on out.

Not to let her relax at her next release, I entered her as her legs trembled and wrapped around my waist. Leaning in and covering her mouth, I sucked her lip for a few minutes and clasped our hands together. Moving slowly at a pace to keep her on edge just a little without going over the cliff, her eyes fluttered open, and she humped me back. My head fell back to hold some type of composure.

"Kyla." I let her hand go and lifted her left leg up for a

deeper angle. I slid down further and felt my chest tighten at the connection.

"I know," she whimpered.

A few more pumps, I adjusted us with her back on top, and I watched her slim finger bounce up and down, staring in my eyes and sucking on my finger at the same time.

"I'm about to come!" she screamed, arching her back.

"Yeah, come for me, baby."

"Yessss! Warren."

⚜

I HADN'T SEEN KYLA SINCE THE NIGHT IN THE CLUB, partially on both our parts. I was in and out for work with Morris. Managing the Vegas opening of the security firm, plus training new team members for the organization left me with limited time for dating anyone. I thanked Esmee and gave her the signed papers for the hiring of new accounts for the Vegas building.

"Anything else before I go?' Esmee asked, standing at the office door. Morris mainly worked out of the club with Mason, and I kept things running here with calls and meetings. He'd built a business that was known around the world as the best security company. No major issues had ever happened on our watch.

Esmee was the office receptionist and annoying little sister that I was glad I never had. She was always trying to tell me what I should be doing with my dating life.

"Nope, you're free to go on your little date."

"Ohh, poor you. Don't be jealous." Esmee chuckled, leaning against the door.

"Nothing to be jealous about." I shrugged, sitting back with my hand behind my head.

Esmee's eyes lowered to slits as she waved her finger in my direction.

"What's going on here? You seem relaxed."

"I'm always relaxed."

"Uhm... I think not." She popped her tongue against her lips.

"Esmee, my life is not your concern."

"Ohh, she must have made an impression."

She started to come back to my office, and I held my hand up.

"I'm not your girlfriend. Gossip somewhere else." I shooed her away.

"Stop being a dork. Who is she?" Esmee shut the door behind her and walked back to sit on top of my desk.

"Nobody." I jumped up, smoothed my tie down, reached for the files on my desk, and headed to my door. I opened the door, jerked back in surprise to see Kyla.

"Sorry, am I interrupting something?" she questioned, looking behind me at Esmee. I looked over my shoulder, and she smirked, trying to reach around me to greet Kyla.

"You're Kyla Stevens! I'm a huge—"

"Esmee, didn't you have some papers to file?"

"No," Esmee responded, reaching out her hand.

Kyla smiled and shook her hand.

"Nice to meet you and thank you," Kyla replied.

"How do you know Mr. Grumpy Pants here?" Esmee pointed at me, and I shoved her out of the office. Kyla giggled as I shut the door in her face.

"Warren!"

"You're fired, Esmee."

"Yeah, yeah... you say that every day," Esmee answered. Kyla burst into laughter.

"What's so funny?" My right brow lifted.

"I like her."

"I don't." I shook my head, motioning for her to take a seat on the couch. I stood against the door as she placed her purse down and crossed her leg.

"I wanted to talk to you about something."

"What's wrong?"

Kyla reached in her purse, and I approached. She opened her email and showed me the email chain of someone talking about how much they love her. They threatened that if she sees me again, they'll expose her with photos from inside Club Seek, plus the time we spent in Vegas together. They had photos of her out shopping, gambling, and even at dinner.

❧ 4 ❧

KYLA

Ever since I came home from Vegas, I thought I could brush off these emails and social media DMs. At first, they were of me out at some industry events, but then it became more of me with my friends and now with Warren. Whoever was stalking me knew my entire day and what time I went to set for filming or out to dinner. I was apprehensive about getting protection, but now the threats were getting too intense.

"How long has this been going on?" Warren went to his desk and picked up his phone. I rushed over and ripped it out of his hands.

"You can't tell anybody."

"Kyla, whoever is doing this is serious."

I held the phone behind my back.

"I only want you to help me."

"What about Morris?"

"Morris is fine, but nobody else."

"I can't promise."

"Warren, this is my life. If this leaks, I'll end up losing my role."

"You can't worry about your career."

"That's easy for you. My career can go away like that." I snapped a finger.

"They know your every move and probably watched you come in here!"

Warren snatched the phone back.

"I knew this was a mistake."

"Let me break it down for you."

He pushed the phone in my face, scrolling over the emails.

kylastevens@gmail.com: Either you leave him alone or find your career gone.

Kylastevens@gmail.com: You think I won't hurt you.

Kylastevens@gmail.com: I loved your scene today.

"My life is going to be over," I groaned, pacing in front of his desk.

He sighed and came around to hug me with his chest to my back.

"Listen to me, I won't let anyone hurt you."

"Warren..."

"Sshhh."

"How can you be so sure?"

"I've trained all my life for this type of work. If having a military background has taught me anything, it's to be diligent at all times."

"Okay."

"I want you to go about your day, and I'll put someone with you."

"Wait... I... I don't want anyone but you." I shuddered.

"Kyla, I can't promise to be with you around the clock."

"Then I don't want security."

"No debate, you're getting security."

"Asshole," I mumbled, moving out of his grip, and started to leave.

"Ah…"

"What?"

"I like this little attitude, princess."

"Shut up."

"All right, I'll do a few shifts, but I can't be with you all the time."

"Fine, it's a deal."

"Where do you need to go now?"

"I wanted to go shopping and then home to study my lines."

"You have girlfriends to do shopping duties."

"Nope, I want you." I gripped his arm, pulled him out of his office, and strolled past his receptionist.

"Bye, Kyla!" she yelled, waving.

"Get back to work!" Warren shouted, holding the door open for me.

"Sure boss," Esmee responded.

❧

Two hours later, I held the candle up to my nose and held it out for Warren to smell. He held a thumbs up.

"I love candles and the fresh aroma in place."

"How much more shopping are you planning to do?"

"Not much longer, a few stores then we can leave."

"You said that about the last five stores."

Warren continued to text while I checked out more candles in Bed, Bath and Beyond. I needed to cleanse my condo after dealing with a stalker for the past few days. Before all of this, I was an open book with my fans and let them hug me, take pictures, and get close. But now, everybody was a suspect unless I knew you personally. I picked up a lavender candle set when my cell rang. I answered to hear my mom fussing in the background.

"Hi, Daddy."

"Hey, baby."

"What's wrong with Momma?"

"The neighborhood boys messed up her flowers."

"Tell her to calm down, otherwise she'll have a heart attack." I chuckled.

"I tried, but you know your mother."

Wendell and Kaitlyn Stevens never lost that charm as a couple and as parents, they always encouraged me to be the best no matter what I wanted to do in life. Even though they would have loved me being a doctor or a lawyer, like any parent, becoming an actress and letting them meet their favorite actors was a bonus for them.

"We wanted to check in with you."

"I'm fine, Daddy."

"Are you sure?"

"Yeah, why?"

"Well, your mother always talks about having these visions or feelings."

I laughed at his statement.

"Daddy, please don't indulge your wife in the crazy."

"Normally I don't."

"But."

"She said she had a feeling you were feeling down."

I looked up at Warren, and we made eye contact. I cleared my throat to figure out the best way to answer my father's words.

"Everything is fine now."

"What does that mean? Is somebody messing with you?"

"Don't freak out."

"Let me determine that."

"I have a stalker," I mumbled lowly.

"A what?"

"Daddy, don't make me say it."

"Mr. Stevens, this is Warren Combs."

I gasped in shock when Warren took the phone.

"Who is this?"

"Kyla's boyfriend."

My mouth gaped open.

"We've just recently made things official, but I can promise that you have nothing to worry about."

"Do I need to come out there?" Dad questioned.

"No, sir. Kyla's in good hands."

"Let me talk to Kyla again."

Warren handed the phone back to me.

"Daddy."

"Who is that guy?"

"Uhm…Warren, he's my boyfriend."

"You make sure you send a picture of him and his driver's license."

I chortled and nodded my head.

"Okay, Daddy. Tell Momma I love her."

"Everything good?" Warren said, wrapping his arm around my shoulder.

"He wants a picture of your face and your driver's license."

"I wouldn't expect anything less."

"I'm hungry now."

"Come on, dinner's on me."

"Can we order in at my place?"

"Sure, lil mama." Warren kissed the side of my face and grabbed my bags.

THIRTY MINUTES LATER, WE MADE IT TO MY HOME. I PUT my things away, ordered seafood takeout, and popped a bottle of wine. I changed into comfy shorts and a t-shirt, and lounged on the couch with *Pink Panther* playing on the screen.

"What made you tell my Dad we're a couple?" I asked.

I had this urge to leave the conversation alone, but the girls would annoy me to no end if they found out before I told them that a one-night stand ended with a relationship.

"Is something wrong with that equation?"

"No, just surprised." I ran a finger around the rim of the glass.

"We're both adults, and I know what I like."

"So, you like me to be your girlfriend."

"I don't make it a habit, but this pull between us won't go away."

"I agree with that, but what about your other women?"

"Probably surprising, but you're the only girl I've had sex with in the last four months."

"Very surprising."

"I'm not some guy who goes around sleeping with people."

"Even being into the club thing?" I gulped the rest of the wine.

"The club doesn't make my dick hard if that's your question."

"What does?"

"You."

We stared at each other for a few minutes.

❧ 5 ❧

KYLA

He fisted my hair, pulled it into a tight ponytail, and stared at me for a moment. He then ran a hand slowly down my chest, and I moaned out. I was so responsive to his touch, the arousal I felt as he bent down and took my left nipple in his mouth ignited my soul on fire.

"Yess... right there." I writhed in his hold, he left my left nipple and twisted my right one.

"You're so beautiful. I could watch you all day."

I gasped at the feel of his warm breath behind my ear. Thinking over how we meshed the other night and then in Vegas, I wondered if this feeling would always be here. Maybe Warren was the person I was missing in my life. Hopefully he knew after his touches, and kisses, it would be tough to leave him alone.

"What do you want to happen tonight?"

Warren turned the video off, helped me out of the shorts, spread my legs wide, and kissed the back of my ankle.

"I should ask you the same thing."

"We can test out how many orgasms you can hold."

"Mmmm..."

"Make it memorable and if you can hold them, I'll reward you."

"With what?" I was in a daze as he sucked on each toe one by one.

My head fell back as I reached down to play with my clit.

"Let me work with her tonight." Warren bent down, spread my lips open, and stuck his tongue inside.

"Warren... oooh."

"I can make you orgasm in one minute."

"It... it's... a bet."

He stuck a finger inside, flicked his tongue across, and lapped up my juices. Then he grabbed the bottle of wine and poured it on my sex and sucked it back up.

"Ahhh!" I cried out.

"That's one."

My leg wrapped around his shoulder, and I gripped his head, humping his face slowly and forgetting about my problems.

"She's sweet, succulent, tight."

Warren raised the bottle to my lips and watched as I took a sip.

"Ughh... please fuck me."

"You can't handle the bet?"

I shook my head no.

"I just want you to fuck me."

He chuckled, rotated his finger, and nibbled along my neck.

"Who fucks you?" he asked.

"You."

"Who am I?"

"My boyfriend!" I screamed, finally understanding his

dominance and command of my body when we were in this position. Warren had a way of awakening certain sexual points I never opened.

"Good. Come with me." Warren extended a hand for me to take.

"Wait... where are we going?"

He picked me up in a bridal style and carried me to my bedroom.

"To fuck."

"But—"

He pushed the first door open and placed me on the bed. After taking off his shirt and pants, he pushed my legs together, held them to the side, and thrusted forward. We both gasped in surprise.

"This belongs to me."

Warren grunted, backed out, and pushed back in, lifting his leg on top of the bed. The position gave me so much more, and I felt the room spinning. His large muscles flexed, and I watched him concentrate so hard, he gritted his teeth.

"Fuck! Baby."

"Yesss... Ughh."

"I promise to keep you safe."

"I know." I teared up, pushing my face in the pillow at his words.

"You need to relax and take this dick," he said, removing the pillows, as he pulled out, turned me on all fours, and slammed back in my entrance.

"Shit!"

"KYLA! KYLA!"

"Huh."

"Did you not hear me?"

"No. What did you say?"

"We're talking about throwing a dinner party for couples," Lisa said.

"Ummm."

Lisa invited us over to her place for lunch and since I didn't need to be on set until later, I agreed. She looked at me funny with a perplexed expression, and I felt like she already knew that Warren and I made things official.

"Couples."

"Yes, Chelsey and Xavier. Maya and Mason, maybe. Me and Morris."

"Just spill."

"What?"

"You know, don't you?"

Lisa held both hands up.

"I hate you."

"You're walking funny, and the off look says your mind is somewhere else."

"I'm dating."

"Someone I know?"

I pushed her, and she cackled.

"Chelsey, I won." Lisa ran in the living room. I followed and watched Chelsey pull out money to pass to Lisa.

"You bet on me."

"She bet you would date him in six months. I bet less than three months." Chelsey laughed and put her purse down on the table.

"I'm going back to California."

"Aww, you know you'll miss us."

"Not likely." I sat next to Chelsey on the couch and crossed my arms.

"She was acting the same way Kyla did when we caught on to her and Morris," Maya said.

"I remember."

"Let's keep my business out of this please," Lisa replied.

"So how is everything going with filming?" Maya questioned.

"Good, besides having a stalker."

The entire room went silent.

"A what?"

"Stalker."

"When did this happen? Did you call the police?" Maya asked.

"Warren is handling things."

"Yep, he spoke with Morris the other day," Lisa said, popping a chip in her mouth.

"You guys tell each other everything," I said.

"The best way to be in a relationship," Lisa answered, grabbing the dip and chips again.

"What type of messages are you getting?" Maya inquired.

"Basically saying I should leave him alone, and they'll expose me if I don't."

"Why are we constantly dealing with crazy people as successful women?" Lisa stated.

"Because people are crazy," Maya answered.

I nodded in agreement.

"Hopefully, it'll get squared away soon."

"If Warren is on the case, you'll be fine," Lisa said.

"Well, let me get out of here. I have call time and need to get going." I rose off the couch, gave each girl a hug, and grabbed my things to leave. Lisa followed and opened the door. I saw my bodyguard waiting at the car that Warren set for me today.

"He's cute at least," Lisa said.

"Don't let Warren hear you say that."

"You know we love those possessive men," Lisa replied.

"So, I shouldn't be crazy that I feel possessive over him?"

"No, girl. Obviously, he's just as interested to already be claiming and making sure you're safe."

"Thanks. I'll call you later."

"Not too late. I might be stuffed." Lisa winked, closing the door in my face, and I rolled my eyes at her craziness.

❧ 6 ❧

KYLA

lashback.

His shirt fell on the floor before he unbuckled his pants and dropped his boxers on the floor. My mouth flew open, seeing something new that wasn't there the first time we had sex.

"I got him pierced," Warren said, walked up on me and grabbed me around the waist, lunging for my lips. The hunger and despair in our movements could be seen by the outside world as two people who had been apart from each other for years instead of a few weeks.

"Can I have you tonight?" he asked.

I nodded.

"I need to hear the words, Miss Stevens."

"Yes."

"Remove your clothes slowly."

He stood back and watched as I kicked my heels off, dragged the skin-tight red cocktail dress off, and dropped it on the floor. Warren walked around me in a circle, scanning my entire body when he gripped me around the waist and pulled my back to his chest. His thick shaft poked at my opening, waiting to enter. He sucked on my neck, and my head fell back as I felt one hand grasp my breast and another cup my sex.

"Once we fuck, you're mine. Do you understand?"

"Uhh..."

"This big motherfucker is going to slide into home."

"Okay."

"So deep, you won't be able to walk afterwards."

"Warren... shit."

His fingers deepened, and the wetness dripped down my legs.

"Let me feel you, Warren."

"At your request."

All of a sudden, I felt empty as he pulled away, until I saw that he grabbed a condom from his wallet.

"Bend over."

He pointed to the couch, and I obeyed and watched him sheath himself as he kicked my legs wider, and pressed his girth at my opening. We both moaned at him being buried so deep. Warren rocked forward, and I gripped the top of the couch and felt the piercing push against my bud.

"Ahhh... This feels good." My tits brushed against the coach, as I bit my bottom lip and ran a hand between my legs to reach his balls as they smacked against my ass.

"Yeah, take control, baby," he said.

"Jesus," I gasped. He moved me away from the couch and had me facing the wall. He told me to touch my toes.

"Tonight, it's just me giving you this good dick," he boasted, smacking me on the ass.

Warren had my pussy leaking and me lightheaded at the same time.

"Don't pass out on me now." He pulled out suddenly, turned me around, and took the condom off before he gripped my hair and pushed his dick in my mouth.

"Shit, Kyla!" he groaned. I masterly fondled his balls as my

tongue swirled around the head. I spat and sucked alongside the vein of his dick.

Present.

"They're ready for you on set," the hairstylist said as she put the brush down and removed the cape. I stood and thanked her, checking myself out in the mirror. The production assistant knocked on the door again.

"I'm coming!"

"One minute, Kyla."

"Time to transport to another world."

"You feeling all right?"

"Why do you ask?"

"You drifted off."

"Long day." I grabbed my script, sauntered out of the trailer, and sat on the cart, while he drove to the sound stage. Today was a night shoot with me and Lee on some intense scenes. Truthfully, I wasn't into working tonight. I wanted to be curled up against Warren again, watching an old 80s film or something while he rubbed my feet. My mother left a voice message to call her when I got a chance. I doubt it'll be tonight.

"Thanks, Cedric."

"No problem, Kyla."

"Quiet on set!" the director shouted. I strolled to the right of him with the camera guy and sound talking over a scene.

"I'm here."

"Hey Kyla, are you ready?" the director questioned.

"Never have to question."

"Tonight, we're going for the jugular," he replied.

"I hear you."

I hugged Lee, dropped my script on the table, stood next to him, and listened as he talked through the scene with me.

"We're ready to film," the director said.

"Places, everybody!" the coordinator told me.

The lights shined on us, and I felt the world outside escape while I looked into Lee's eyes and became my character again.

"Action."

"I want a divorce," Lee spoke, turning his back to me.

"Divorce! How dare you."

"We've known this has been over and moved on."

"Who? Who have you moved on with?"

"Not that it matters."

"Cut. I want a little closer to Kyla's face," the director said to the camera operator.

⬥

FILMING FINISHED FIFTEEN MINUTES AGO, AND I STARTED to walk out of the building to the parking lot, when a guy wearing blue jeans and a leather jacket approached me, holding flowers.

"Kyla." He held the flowers out to me.

"I'm sorry, do I know you?"

"These are for you."

"Who are they from?"

"A secret admirer."

"Sorry, I can't take them."

"Why not?"

"Because I don't know you. How did you get inside here?"

"Don't worry about that."

I tried to walk around him, but he gripped my arm.

"It's flowers. What's the big deal?"

"Let my arm go."

"Bitch," he spat and threw the flowers on the ground

and stomped away mad. I ran to the car and saw the body-guard asleep at the wheel. I banged on the window, and he woke up startled.

"That's him!" I pointed to the guy driving off in his car.

"What? Who?"

"The stalker. Go follow him."

"Let me call Warren."

"He's getting away!" I yelled, reaching in my purse to dial Warren.

"Calm down. I'll handle things." He turned the car on and drove off, but the guy was long gone by the time we left the parking lot. Twenty minutes later, we ended up at Warren's place, and I fired the guy and told him to leave. Warren stood at the door with a harsh glare on his face. I made it to the door, and he pulled me inside and roamed over my body to check for any wounds.

"Warren."

"Did he touch you?"

"No, I promise. I'm fine."

"Okay, come here." He hugged me close, tight in his grip.

"I can't breathe."

"Sorry, come sit."

"Did you fire him?"

"Yeah. Did you get a good look at the guy?"

"He was young looking, beady eyes, thin lips, freckled face."

"I don't think he's the guy."

"What do you mean?"

"He wouldn't have approached you so soon."

"Why do you say that?"

"The guy tonight was probably a regular fan, but your stalker was too familiar with me."

"So."

"I think it's about me."

"Someone is trying to get to you through me?"

He walked me to the couch, then went over to the bar and poured a drink for me. I gulped the whiskey down and it burned my throat, then held the glass out for another shot.

"Slow down on those now."

"After tonight, I can handle a bottle."

"Tonight, you'll sleep here."

"Sounds good."

❄ 7 ❄

WARREN

Two days later, I sat with the guys at the bar to grab some drinks after a long day of work, while guarding Kyla at her film shoot. Morris ordered a round of drinks, and I finished off my second before ordering a third.

"Lisa said Kyla's been with you lately at your place."

"We split between my place and hers."

"Any clues on the stalker?"

"Not really."

"You need more people on her?"

"At the moment, no, but if I go out of town, I'll let you know."

"Gentlemen, who wants to lose to me in a round of pool?" Mason asked.

"Rack them up," Morris said. I watched them place money on the table to bet.

"Xavier, how's the fitness business coming along?" I asked.

He popped the top on the beer bottle and chugged it down.

"Busy, which makes me think we might need to get security," Xavier said.

"Let Morris know, and we'll set up a meeting."

"Chelsey insists I hire a manager and spend more time with her."

"How long have you two been together?"

"A year," he replied, waving for the waitress to bring another round. Mason cursed when Morris made a score.

"No kids?"

"Not yet. Still in the honeymoon stage."

"I feel you on that. Kyla and I are the same."

"We've known each other all our lives."

I chuckled.

"I guess Chelsey waited for you to make a move."

"Actually, she made the first move."

"She's a boss."

"Yeah, Peanut keeps me on my toes."

"Peanut?"

"She hates that name, so don't tell her."

"No worries."

"Chelsey told me about some stalker."

"Kyla has a stalker, but I think it's a scare tactic."

"For what?"

"To get to me."

"Be careful."

"I plan to."

"Let's play teams!" Morris shouted.

"He's already wasted; you have him on your team," I said.

"He's the worst player. I'll pay you to be his partner."

We both laughed, and Morris flipped us both off. I grabbed a stick and played three rounds before ordering more beer. My phone vibrated, and I pulled it out to see Kyla messaged me.

"Miss you."

"Miss you more."

"Enough to come here and suck my pussy?"

"Don't tempt me."

"Tease, tempt, whatever works."

"Get off your phone!" Morris barked.

"Drink some water and sober up," I fussed back and leaned against the pool table. "I have a surprise for you," she texted.

"Let me see."

"You have to come and get it."

"On my way to you."

"I'm at your place."

"I thought... On my way."

"Stop wussing out and play," Morris said.

"Gotta go. My baby is waiting on me," I said.

෴

I DROPPED MY POOL STICK ON THE TABLE, TOOK MONEY out of my wallet, and grabbed the bottle of water to sober up enough to drive. Thirty minutes later, I arrived home, slid the key in the door, and called out for Kyla. The living room was dark with candles lit around the room, and I smiled, thinking about our time at the mall when she bought up all the candles.

I took off my jacket, kicked my shoes off and went to my bedroom. When I pushed the door open, I saw the last person I would expect lying on my bed.

"Hey, baby."

"Esmee." I shut the door behind me and walked further in the room.

"Come to bed." She held her hand out for me.

"You've been sending those messages."

"What messages?" She sat up on her knees, wearing only a robe and bra set.

"Have you been emailing Kyla?"

Her facial expression went sour.

"I don't want to talk about her."

"Why not?" I approached her and touched her cheek. I ran a finger across her lips, down to her throat, and gripped her around the neck.

"I... I... can't breathe."

"Why?"

"Please, Warren."

"Tell me the truth." I lightened my grip around her neck.

"She doesn't love you like I do," Esmee whimpered, wiping the tears from her cheek.

"Cut the shit."

"Please, Warren, I've loved you since the day you hired me two years ago."

"Too bad. I don't want you. Get dressed."

"No, that bitch has money, looks, and a career. Let her find her own man."

"You sound stupid right now."

"We are meant to be together."

Bang! Bang!

"Get dressed."

"Is that your little whore?" Esmee got out of bed and started to walk to the front door. I pushed her back and pointed to her clothes.

"Get dressed, or I'm calling the police," I said, left the room, and jogged to the door. I looked out the window to see Morris and Xavier.

"You forgot your money." Morris held out a hundred bucks.

"Glad you're here."

"Warren, we need to talk about this." Esmee came out of my room, causing Morris and Xavier to glare at me.

"She's the stalker," I said.

"What!" Morris and Xavier said at the same time.

"He's lying." Esmee tried to wiggle out of my arms, and I grasped her arm harder.

"Check her phone in her purse, Xavier."

I took it out of her hands and threw it to him, watching her fidget around nervously.

"She has an app downloaded to block out her number." Xavier held her cell up with pictures and text threads of Kyla coming and going around the city and to work.

"You don't understand." Esmee reached over to place her hand on my chest, and I smacked it down.

"Why?" Morris demanded, taking out his phone. I heard him calling the police.

"I love you, Warren, and she doesn't deserve you."

"We work together, nothing more or less."

"That's not true! We have the same interests, and I know you want me," Esmee explained. My thoughts ran around in my head. Many times, we'd work late together, or I'd have her fly with me back and forth to Vegas, but it was never any type of dating in my mind. I always thought of her as a friend.

"The police are on the way," Morris said.

"How did you know about the club?"

"I followed her," Esmee mentioned lowly.

"Did you send that guy to deliver the flowers?" I needed to find out as many details as possible before the police arrested her.

She nodded and wiped her tears.

"But we can be together, Warren. I know you better than she will ever know you," Esmee declared. Morris moved out of the way when two officers approached my door.

"Call Kyla," Morris said.

The officers talked with Xavier, taking notes. Another officer took Esmee off my hands.

"No! I love you, Warren. Why are you doing this!" she screamed.

"How long has this been going on?" the officer asked me.

I ran a hand down my face, sighed in disgust at the person I'd been working alongside in my presence. I remembered Kyla meeting Esmee, and she seemed cool and starstruck, but all along, she was envious and wanted to ruin her career and life over me.

"She's been stalking my girlfriend."

"All right, you'll need to come down to the station, and your girlfriend, for a statement."

"Please, Warren! I'll leave her alone if you promise to love me," Esmee cried, fighting to get out of the handcuffs.

"This is crazy." I slid my hands in my pants pockets, watching them push Esmee in the police car.

"Glad it ended with Kyla not getting hurt," Morris said.

"I need to call her."

❦   8   ❦

WARREN

A week later.

Kyla placed her hands on my chest and straddled me, showing her tight, sexy lips that I couldn't wait to suck, and fuck until we both passed out. I let her move at her own pace instead of controlling tonight. I knew she'd had a shitty week with getting a restraining order on Esmee and keeping her career afloat. She pushed her breasts in my face, and I used my free hand to pinch and tease her nipples, as I sucked her sexy, chocolate areola in my mouth. I deliberately did it slowly and watched her eyes lower as lust showered over her face.

"I want you to fuck my breasts," she said, nudging them out of my mouth, and crawling down and removing my underwear. She picked up my stiff shaft, put it between her tits, and stuck her tongue out to lick the tip.

"Shit, Kyla, don't play with it."

"I want you to come on my face."

Those words sparked a fire in my belly. She'd said I changed her in ways, but she did the same for me. My only mission was to keep a smile on her face. Thrusting upwards, she continued to lick and suck while her breasts cupped my dick.

"Fuck!" I growled and came a second later. I was still hard, and she climbed back over me and sunk down on my waist, bouncing up and down. I gripped her around the waist to help control her movement. The sounds in her bedroom got louder. Her lips moved toward me and trailed kisses to my chin and behind my ear. She knew that was my spot, and I growled feeling myself get heated in embarrassment.

"I'll make you pay for that."

She giggled as I flipped us over and pushed her legs back to her chest as I buried my face in her neck.

"Aghhh! Warren, you're so deep."

"This fat pussy can handle it, right?"

I taunted, switched my strokes from fast to slow, then went in a circular motion. She rubbed her clit, shuddered beneath me, and I knew she was about to come.

"What do you want, Kyla?"

"You!" she screamed. I maneuvered, let her legs wrap around my waist, slowed my strokes, and made love to her slowly, tenderly letting my release come inside her. I rolled off her to catch my breath, and she threw her leg over mine and kissed along my chest.

"I'm not the least bit scared of where this goes between us," she said.

I rubbed up and down her back, cupped her ass, and pecked her on the lips.

"So, we're a couple?"

"Are you cool with that? The spotlight I mean?"

"As long as we're together, I'm fine. Just be honest with me."

Kyla smirked, leaned over, and licked my neck, causing my dick to stand at attention. She went over to the drawer and grabbed the bottle bullet I thought I threw away and turned it on.

"What are you about to do with that?"

"How about a little sixty-nine before bed?" She passed the bullet to me and reversed around with her face over my dick and ass in my face. I smacked and spread her ass cheeks, and swiped my tongue from top to bottom.

"First one to come has to make dinner."

"Shit, I'll buy your dinner and breakfast if I can get this tight ass again."

I put the bullet to her lips, and she moaned, grabbing my dick.

"Baby," she weakly grumbled, her body shivering and convulsing under my touch. The sounds of her coming back to back spearheaded me to fit her snug walls again as the loud smacking in the room would capture our pleasure.

❦

A DAY LATER.

I walked next to Kyla in the grocery store while she ran off each item she needed for dinner. I loved when she was just plain Kyla dressed down in jeans, Vans, and an oversized t-shirt she took from my closet.

"What do you think of kale salad, baked chicken, and mixed veggies?"

I pushed the cart and stopped in front of the frozen food aisle. She bent over to grab a bag and toss it in the basket.

"That's fine with me."

"Perfect, have you heard anything from you know who?"

My phone would get random calls from an unknown number, and I figured it was Esmee trying to reach out, but I blocked her every time. When I went to visit her, I told her to never contact me again or Kyla if she didn't want more charges brought up.

FLASHBACK BEFORE VEGAS.

"What are you doing?" Esmee asked me and dropped our food on the desk. It was a busy day around the office, and I couldn't leave when I had to hire and get the estimates on the amount of team members to hire over to Barry.

"What do you know about Kyla Stevens?" I closed out the gossip blogs on my computer and went back to the payroll template before she could see my screen.

"She's an actress, why?"

"Nothing major."

"You see celebrities all the time. What's the big deal?"

"No big deal. I just met her the other day with Morris."

"Interesting."

"What does interesting mean?" I sat back in my chair and picked up the spicy rice and chicken from the Jamaican restaurant near the office.

"You don't seem like the groupie type."

I scrunched my nose.

"Groupie."

"I just expected you to be into more of a classier woman."

"Like who?"

"Don't take this the wrong way, but I seem more of your speed than Kyla," Esmee said.

Present.

"Are you listening to me?" Kyla asked.

"Huh."

"I asked, how did the visit go with Esmee?"

"Nothing you have to worry about."

Kyla looked at me and nodded.

"What?"

"You make me happy, that's all."

"My job, lil mama."

"Kyla Stevens! It's really you. Can I have an autograph?" A young woman approached us with her camera and note-book in her hand. I took the camera out of her hand, and Kyla mouthed thank you and stood next to her and signed her name. After taking the picture, we continued grocery shopping and packed the car up. I held the passenger door open for her to climb in, shut the door, and went to the driver's side. My phone vibrated, and I saw a number I didn't know.

Unknown: She'll never be me.

Deleting the message, I slid the key in the ignition and drove back home. We arrived fifteen minutes later and unpacked the food. I sat watching her around my kitchen, getting things prepared and talking about her upcoming premiere and my trip out of town for work.

The bedroom door pushed open, and my mom walked in with Lisa and Chelsey behind her in their best outfits. The premiere was today, and I was excited to finally walk the red carpet and meet some of my supportive fans. Warren had to fly out to Vegas to handle business with the security firm, so the girls were my escorts tonight. Chelsey wore a floral gown with red gladiator shoes to match and wide pockets on the side. Lisa's outfit was just as pretty, showing her curves and fashionable taste in a baby-blue pantsuit and no bra. Red lipstick made the entire outfit pop. I smiled and stood, reaching out to hug them both while still wearing my robe.

"Are you almost ready, Ky?" Mom asked.

"Give me ten more minutes, Mom."

Lisa handed me a gift bag, and I pursed my lips.

"What did you do? I said no gifts."

"I know, but you deserve it after all the mess I got you involved in with the club," Lisa replied.

"Stop blaming yourself. I'm a grown woman, and I made my choices."

"She's right, Lisa. We all decided to join the club," Chelsey stated, holding a black gift bag.

"You two."

I shook my head, sat on the edge of the bed, and opened Lisa's gift first. I burst into laughter.

"I'll wait outside," Mom said, and all three of us laughed. Just like Lisa to gift me a taser for protection.

"What am I going to do with this?" I turned it around and rolled my eyes at the pink taser case in the bag.

"Duh, protection."

"I have Warren for that." I removed the wrapping paper from Chelsey's gift bag and giggled at the silver cuffs with the pink ruffled cover around them. I chuckled at both girls always thinking outside the box when it came to gifts. I stuffed everything back in the bags and stood to hug Lisa and Chelsey.

"Are you ready for your big premiere?" Lisa asked, checking herself out in the vanity mirror. I stepped out of my robe, wearing only a strapless bra and thong set. I treaded over to the bathroom, took my yellow canary dress off the back of the door, and slipped it over my head.

"Yes, and soon as we finish, I need to eat."

I nudged Lisa to move over and finished touching up my makeup, grabbed my purse and keys, and looked around the room to make sure I didn't miss anything.

"All right, ladies. It's time!" I squealed, clapping my hands together in excitement.

Lisa led the way out of my room, down the hall to my mom and dad waiting on us to head out to the limo.

"Ky... you are so beautiful, baby." Dad leaned over to peck me on the cheek.

"Thanks, Daddy."

My publicist ended her call, grinning at me.

"You ready?" she questioned.

"More than ready."

She hugged me, then looked me over, and gave me a thumbs up.

"You'll walk the red carpet and take a few questions," Janell informed me, texting away on her phone.

"Nothing about my personal life, Janell." I nodded at the driver. He held the door open for us to climb in, and I scooted in after my mom.

"They already know. Don't worry, today is your day," Janell replied and pushed her phone in front of my face to show me trending on social media.

"Stop stressing, Kyla. You have the man, the career, and family," Lisa reminded me and cuffed my palm to squeeze.

❧

"Kyla, who are you wearing today?" the reporter asked.

I looked down at my dress and back up at the reporters as the cameras flashed.

"I'm wearing Diane Von Furstenberg."

More shutter clicks went off at my revelation. Some actors loved the red carpet, but I found it so exhausting and boring to constantly answer the same questions over and over again.

"Kyla has more questions to answer. Thanks, guys." Janell ushered me away to the next row of reporters. I posed with my mom and dad, then Lisa and Chelsey for a few more poses. I then waved to some fans waiting. I smiled while heading toward the doors of the theater. I was completely thrown off at Warren in a nice button-down jacket, black slacks, and dreads pulled to the back, showing off his shaped-up beard.

"What... How..." I was speechless, as tears pooled in my eyes.

He pulled me to his chest in front of the whole world, causing every reporter and photographer to film us.

"I took a flight to get back here in time."

"But I thought you needed to stay to cover for Morris."

Warren grinned and bent down to kiss my forehead.

"Everything is fine at the office; you're more important," Warren said.

"Thank you."

"No reason to thank me, lil mamma."

"Never had a guy go out of his way to do something this big for me."

"Stick with me, and you'll get something else big," he growled and kissed the side of my neck. I shook my head and stepped out of his arms.

"Save that for later."

"Warren, nice to finally meet you in person. My daughter speaks so highly of you all the time." Mom let my dad's arm go and hugged him. Warren greeted my dad, then the girls, while Janell led us into the movie theater.

"Excuse me, Kyla Stevens?" A guy, around five-ten, with low cut, black spiky hair, wearing a t-shirt with my name across it, walked up on me.

"Yes."

Warren tightened his grip around my waist and pulled me behind him, to put space between me and the gentleman.

"I think we all have some alpha men, but sweet at the same time," Lisa whispered for only me and Chelsey to hear.

"We have Maya to blame." I giggled, remembering how this all started by one invitation into a sex club that handled all of your desires.

"I'm a huge fan. Can I have an autograph?" he asked.

"Sure, baby. It's fine." I rubbed Warren's arm to relax him.

I grabbed the pen from the guy's hand, signed his picture, and thanked him.

"Thank you," he said, strolling out of the theater.

"I'm still getting used to that," Warren said.

"Used to what?"

"You being some big celebrity."

"Awww, you're sweet. But I'm just Kyla."

He placed a finger under my chin and stared into my eyes.

"To me, you're my heartbeat."

"I guess it was a good idea."

"What was?"

"Vegas."

"Anytime you want to go back, I have more toys for you." Warren winked and grasped my hand.

"Good, because I have a few of my own."

EPILOGUE: KYLA

Six months later.

My eyes watched as the scowl across his face deepened, and I wondered if we'd ever get to that happy place. How long had I been afraid, nervous, nauseous that this love wouldn't be enough for him? I looked away, turned silently, and wept as he wrapped his arms around my waist and held me close.

"Cut!" the director yelled, and everyone clapped in excitement at wrapping season two on a new project with me as the lead. After the premiere of my last leading role, I had to fly out to California for six months to film a secret project that would be airing in a year. My schedule only got busier with film studios wanting to work with me, calling my agent to send me scripts and audition. I missed my girls, but we talked on FaceTime a lot, and I told them I'd be back to Tennessee to visit as soon as things wrapped up here.

"Kyla, once again, you amazed me." Lee went to hug me, and I reciprocated. Our chemistry was off the chain, and he was a great sparring partner that I would miss acting with, but I knew our paths would cross again when the final product came around.

"Thanks, Lee. You weren't too bad yourself," I joked, and he blushed.

"Baby, you ready?" Warren came up beside me and kissed me on the cheek, and I smiled. To think he'd become my personal bodyguard on top of being my man for these last few months.

"Yes, I'm just finishing up with Lee." I motioned at him.

"Warren, did you get my email about the club opening?" Lee asked, and I was glad to hook Warren up with more clients. Lee invested in a club with his brother and needed help getting security, so I recommended Morris' company. Warren was taking the day-to-day lead over Vegas and West Coast in general.

"I have my people working on sending you the details," Warren replied.

"Great, you guys should come to the opening," Lee suggested and left the set. Warren followed me to my dressing room. Opening the door, I stepped in and sat on the couch.

"Super star, how does it feel?"

Warren bent down, removed my shoes, and sat next to me with my legs in his lap.

"Feels great."

"Good, you deserve it."

"What are your plans now that filming is finished?"

I sat up and straddled his lap, extending my arms around his neck. He palmed my butt. I took in his open chest in the black Ralph Lauren shirt that clung to his body, rubbing my hand up his chest.

"How about I go with you back to Memphis for good?"

"Are you saying you want to move permanently?" His brow raised.

"I am. What do you think about us living together?"

Warren ran a hand up and down my back.

"I'm ready."

"The best is yet to come." He smirked, flipped me on my back, and pressed kisses all over my face as I giggled at him roaming a hand around my body.

"Thank you for protecting me, Warren."

"You don't have to thank me, Kyla."

Our lips glued together, and my tongue rubbed over his bottom lip, pushing through it.

"You let me bare my soul and didn't run away."

❦

I HOPE YOU ENJOYED KYLA AND WARREN'S STORY. DID I forget to mention Xavier and Chelsey with "**Seek To Love Book 4**" is here https://books2read.com/u/mB2QvO

Check out Brother's BestFriend Romance here ***"Sensual"*** https://books2read.com/u/49lYYM

Don't miss out on ***"Love Don't Live here Anymore book 1"*** https://books2read.com/u/mBOWGZ a steamy enemies to lovers romance.

Have you checked out **"His Peace Her Pleasure"** click here https://books2read.com/u/3JJroP a billionaire, steamy romance.

BONUS CONTENT: KYLA

The camera was rolling. All my life, I'd waited for this moment and couldn't believe it was finally happening. Each clip was played and showcased our best scenes that we provided when the presenter opened the envelope. I held my breath and clenched Warren's hand next to me with a knot in my stomach.

"The Emmy goes to Kyla Stevens!" she announced, and tears poured from my eyes. I reached over and hugged Warren tight, ruining my makeup, but I didn't care. Moments like this made it worth the late night and long hours of filming to see my name up in lights next to the big actors in Hollywood. I was an Emmy-winning actress, starring in the next big blockbuster film, dating a man who loved and protected me for the last year. I sauntered up on stage, grabbed the award, and thanked them.

"Wow!"

The audience clapped and cheered for me as I smiled in excitement.

"Thank you so much. I couldn't have done this without my family and friends. Especially you, Warren."

He smirked and mouthed 'I love you.'

"This has been a long journey, but I wouldn't want anyone else with me."

I turned the recording off after watching it several times and grabbed the champagne Lisa poured. We all sat around the front of the yacht, listening to music and lounging in our bikinis. Going back to that day and night was epic and overshadowed the bad things that tried to cause me harm. Esmee was sentenced to ten years in prison and ordered to stay away from Warren and me for life if she got out on parole. We had a restraining order still because she'd call from different numbers from time to time.

"To many more vacations like this," Lisa toasted, sipping on her drink.

"I love it out here," Chelsey remarked, looking around the ocean as we sailed through Morocco

"Me too."

"Where are the boys?" Lisa asked.

"Probably drinking and gambling below deck."

"So, who's having a kid next?" Maya questioned. Lisa and I glanced at each other, then pointed toward Chelsey.

"No kids over here, maybe in ten years," Lisa replied.

"Same. I want to do more traveling and filming, maybe Broadway," I said. They all raised their glasses and cheered me on.

304 PUBLISHING COMPANY

WE SHOWCASE AUTHORS writing African American, Interracial, Women's Fiction, Urban Romance, Erotic, and Contemporary Romance novels. Along with Thriller, Suspense, Poetry, Beauty, and Style Books. Thank you for taking the time out to visit. Join our mailing list to stay updated with new releases and blog posts.

WHAT'S NEXT

WANT TO KNOW WHAT HAPPENS next?

Follow me on Bookbub and social media today.

Reviews are the lifeblood of the publishing world. They're read, appreciated, and needed. Please consider taking the time to leave a few words on wherever you buy books. Sign up for updates and sneak peeks at the site below.

CATALOGUE OF RELEASES BY
KEKE RENÉE:

Catalogue of Releases by Keke Renée:

•Wet Heat (Wet Heat Series Book 1)

•Every Time We Touch Novelette (Wet Heat Book 2 Series)

•His Peace, Her Pleasure

•Baby, It's Cold Outside

•Love Don't Live Here Anymore, Vanessa Andrew Book 1

•Love Don't Live Here Anymore, Isabella Andrew Book 2

•One Night Only-A Novelette (Love by Design Book 1)

•Cassian and Savannah (Love by Design Book 2)

•Deidra's Love (Love by Design Book 3)

•Protecting Bria (Special Force Operation Alphas)

Thank you so much for reading.

If you enjoyed the crazy ride and decide to leave a review, we'd appreciate the support.

I WANT TO THANK FIRST readers for loving these characters so much and waited so love for them to come back.

ACKNOWLEDGMENTS

I CAN'T MENTION ENOUGH the support and dedication of my author buddies for keeping me uplifted. My behind-the-scenes team of beta readers, editors, designers, and more. As a writer, I continue to strive for the best, and I appreciate everyone who reads my work. Without your continual feedback, I wouldn't be on this path, letting doubts slip away.

9 7 9 8 2 0 1 5 0 9 5 3 8